Souvenirs
And Other Stories

Matt Tompkins

Conium Press
Portland, OR

"With his new collection *Souvenirs*, Matt Tompkins again shows his ability to tap into a certain loneliness in unique and fascinating ways. In each of these stories, Tompkins creates unusual circumstances and then drops unsuspecting characters directly in the middle of them. The results are sometimes hilarious, often heartbreaking, and always profound. No one else today is plumbing the depths of the human spirit and its limits in quite the same way as Tompkins. *Souvenirs*, in the most inventive way possible, is more a collections of hearts than stories, more a gathering of souls than mere words."

—Sheldon Lee Compton,
author of *Brown Bottle*

"Matt Tompkins is a master of blending surreal circumstances with a deeply human sense of longing. These characters, whether they are grappling with the family of mountain lions living in their basement, a botched Lasik surgery which left one poor chap seeing flames, or a father who has evaporated and reappears in the water supply, are characters you root for. Tompkins creates a collection reminiscent of a quirky, yet lovable mixture of the likes of Harvey Pekar and Aimee Bender. *Souvenirs and Other Stories* is a strange, heartbreaking, and often darkly comical book."

—Beth Gilstrap,
author of *I Am Barbarella*

Souvenirs
And Other Stories

Matt Tompkins

Conium Press
Portland, OR

Souvenirs and Other Stories,
by Matt Tompkins
Published in the United States of America by Conium Press
Portland, Oregon
http://www.coniumreview.com
© 2016 Matt Tompkins & Conium Press

ISBN-10 1-942387-06-7
ISBN-13 978-1-942387-06-0
Library of Congress Control Number: 2016941404

Cover Typefaces: "Chrysalis" & "Chrysalis Filled" (version 1.0)
from Ben McGehee / UA Type
Cover Images: © ivook / Dollar Photo Club
Cover Design: James R. Gapinski & Uma Rallabhandi
Layout: James R. Gapinski
Copy Editing: James R. Gapinski

Contents

THE WATER CYCLE

When I was twelve years old, my dad evaporated. He'd been sitting in his ratty recliner reading the newspaper. I was across the living room, cross-legged on our old corduroy couch. I looked up from my *Fantastic Four* and he was—how do I put it?—he was somehow even less present, less *there*, than usual.

It started with his thinning, bark-brown hair—the same hair that I inherited. It grew wispier still as it wafted away. This evaporative process continued until his plaid sweater vest, pleated khakis, pair of socks, were empty. They all just deflated, laid out flat on the still-reclined lounger. His newspaper slumped like a crumpled pup tent over top.

To be fair, my dad was always kind of airy. He was perpetually distracted. He was prone to daydream. But this was different.

A moment later, he regrouped—re-formed as a fog in the air above his chair. Then, slowly but steadily, he drifted downward, and disappeared: sucked into the belly of the dehumidifier that ran year-round to keep the house from molding.

Late that afternoon, my mom came home. Despite my loud and tearful protests, she pulled the bucket from the dehumidifier. She walked it, sloshing, out to the garage and then dumped it unceremoniously down the throat of the utility sink.

And so my dad became a fully-integrated part of the Odsburg Municipal Sanitary Water System. I had learned all about this from Mrs. Wilkins in Science class. My father would now be undergoing filtration, chlorination, and fluoridation. Then he would be pumped into a reservoir—from whence he could flow to who-knows-where within the county—to be drank, bathed in, used for washing clothes or cars or dishes, or even to fill a toilet. In any case, he'd be washed back into one drain or another, to repeat the process all over again.

Of course, there was another possibility: that he would escape. That he would break free of the open circuit that is the municipal water system. That he would become instead a part of the greater Water Cycle—the one Mother Nature put into motion billions of years ago. We had learned about this, too.

Ways to make the transition are many and varied. They include, but are not limited to: running out of a garden hose and into the ground; becoming a puddle (as a byproduct of car-washing, lawn sprinkling, etc.); evaporating from a wash basin or water glass near an open window; finding oneself in a dog dish and managing to be escorted outside as a trail of slobber; being splashed from a kiddie pool, water balloon, or squeegee bucket; and the list goes on—and on and on. There are frankly too many possibilities to mention. Ultimately, by one means or another, my dad did make it out. I know because he came back to see me.

The first time, he was a wave on Lake Ogannon. I was wading chest-deep in the shallows, splashing around. He rolled directly toward me and broke just a few feet short of my face. I knew it was him because it was just exactly his corny, dad-like sense of humor: to wave to me as a wave. I could almost hear his voice: "Son, look: I'm waving!" My mom was nearby on the shore, reading a book, but I didn't bother to call out to her. She gave me the strangest looks and talked about doctors any time I talked about my dad.

The next time, he was a cloud. I couldn't think of how to say hi to him, or to let him know I saw him there. He was so high up and I was all the way down on the ground. I got so sad about it that I started crying. That turned out to be pretty perfect, actually. My tears evaporated, and rose up to join him in the sky. Then I think neither of us felt quite as lonely or as sad.

The last time was just a few weeks ago. He must've found his way back into the city water system, because he turned up in my coffee. I think this might have been his idea of a practical joke. Once I spotted him, I couldn't bring myself to drink the coffee. Not that I think he would have particularly minded, but it was just a little too weird. I mean, it's one thing to slap a puddle high-five; it's another thing entirely to cannibalize your father. So instead I ate the rest of my breakfast and left him sitting there in the mug. When I was done eating, I told him a little bit about my week. The wife and kids were already gone, to work and to school, so it was only the two of us. It was nice to just sit and spend some time together—me and my dad.

Sometimes, I wonder if I should be angrier

at him for disappearing. People have suggested it often enough—my mom, my friends, my therapist. But somehow, I don't blame him—or, rather, I don't see the use in holding a grudge. He probably lost as much as I did when he went away, maybe more. And anyway, how much choice did he have—how much say in the way he behaved? Maybe we're just slaves to our nature. Maybe I shouldn't make excuses for him, though. Maybe it's just easier to tell myself he didn't *choose* to leave us.

Before long, I had to leave. The GroceryPlus produce section was not going to stock and inventory itself. On my way out the door, I poured my dad into the flowerbed. That way he's free to go about his business, and I know he'll find his way back when he can. In the meantime, I thought, who would want to be stuck inside a coffee mug all day?

If it ever comes to it—and let's face it, maybe someday it will—I hope my kids will have the decency to do the same for me.

Seeking Advice and/or Assistance Re: Mountain Lions

Yes, so.

There's a family of mountain lions living in my basement.

I say *a family* because I know there's more than one, but I don't know exactly how many. If I knew how many, I'd just give you the hard number. Like *five mountain lions*. But that would only be a guess.

To be fair, a *family* of mountain lions may not be correct either. I'm not sure they're related. To be really precise, then: there is a *group* of mountain lions living in my basement. And in case you're wondering, there's no proper term for a group of mountain lions. I looked it up.

Not a herd, or a pack, or a gaggle, or a pride—

not even a murder, as it is with crows, and which I personally think would be apt! (Please notice that I've not yet entirely lost my sense of humor.)

Anyway, apparently, they (mountain lions) typically fly solo. Solitary beasts. So no one ever bothered to name a group. What I want to know, then, is how I managed to get so lucky. A whole group of them in *my* basement! I'm being facetious, if you couldn't tell, about the luck.

A note seems in order here, about planning. I did plan to have my house custom-built. I did not plan to have mountain lions living in my basement. Even though I only planned one of these, both things happened. I suppose that goes to show you can't plan for everything. That is what I call a *lesson for life*.

It's a real beauty of a house, by the way. Three beds, two baths, open floor plans. In a desirable neighborhood with good schools. Took out a sizable loan from the credit union to finance it. Thirty-year mortgage, but worth it. That's what I kept telling myself.

During construction I stopped by every week just to see how it was progressing. One day, I noticed that the foundation was open, exposed to the elements, while the construction crew framed and walled the main structure of the house. It occurred to me that if it rained during this time, water would get into the foundation. I said something to the foreman about this and he said not to worry, they had it all under control. Then he waved me off like a fly. Told me to relax: leave it to the experts.

But do you know what did not occur to me when I saw the gaping foundation? That a group of mountain lions might nest in the basement. So I didn't say anything about that. My mistake, I suppose.

They must have come down from the hills north of the village. The mountain lions, that is. Not the construction workers. The construction workers came from Graysville, two towns over.

I didn't even know the hills had mountain lions living in them.

But I guess they do.

Anyhow, wherever the mountain lions came from, now they're in my basement. Let me restate for the record: the possibility of this happening did not occur to me. It simply did not occur. Apparently, it did not occur to the construction foreman either. Or to any construction foreman, ever. Or to the people who wrote the building codes. There's nothing on the books about it at all. The foreman insists that, for these reasons, he's not liable. He says he followed standard procedure. He says this is my problem alone. He also said they had everything under control. I guess maybe that's just an expression.

Still, whoever may or may not be liable, there are mountain lions in my basement. And I'll tell you something else: I didn't even know they were there. Not at first. Not for a while. That may sound silly. You may wonder how one could overlook a group of mountain lions. Well, I'll tell you how. It was winter when we moved into the house and the mountain lions must have been sleeping very deeply. Taking a long winter's nap. You'll notice that I didn't say *hibernating*. The word choice was intentional. According to my research, mountain lions don't hibernate.

Call it what you will, then. Sleeping. Napping. Snoozing. Lying in wait. Whatever. They were down there in the basement, quiet and unmoving, for months. At any rate, when spring came, the mountain lions awoke.

They must have been hungry then. They started scratching at the basement door. What could that be, I thought to myself when I heard the scratching. I didn't know yet that it was mountain lions. I peeked through the narrow gap underneath the door. I saw big tan paws and sharp claws and fangs and fur and whiskers and several large pink noses. When I put all this together, I had my answer.

14 | Seeking Advice and/or Assistance re: Mountain Lions

It was mountain lions.

The mountain lions were scratching from the inside-the-basement side, where they were. I could hear them from the other side, the outside-of-the-basement side, where I was. So at least we were on opposite sides of the door, me and the mountain lions. I guess that's what you call a *silver lining*.

They were also snuffling, which was quieter than the scratching, but still audible. It made me feel weird to think that they were smelling me. When I say *weird* I suppose I really mean *terrified*.

I first heard the mountain lions when I was in the kitchen, where the basement door leads into. I noticed I could also hear them from my bedroom when I tried to go to sleep that night. My bedroom is on the second floor, which means they were scratching pretty loudly. My wife and our baby son were both scared. My wife was scared of the idea of being mauled by mountain lions. My baby son was just scared of the unfamiliar scratching sound. He is too young to know what mauling is, or what mountain lions are. Another silver lining.

To address the scratching, I went to the garage and got a saw. I used the saw to cut a narrow slot in the basement door. The slot is for sliding raw steaks into. The raw steaks are for feeding the mountain lions. The feeding is so they would hopefully calm down and stop scratching.

After all, the wooden door wouldn't stand up to all that scratching forever. I mean, sure, it's solid hardwood—really high-end construction— but come on: those multiple sets of four-inch claws, working day and night? Piles of the rich blond wood shavings had begun to collect and grow larger on the threshold. A hedgerow of teeny haystacks.

I'm not so sure about that image: haystacks. That makes it sound quaint, pastoral. It's not. It's eerie. Chilling, even. And the math behind it so brutally simple: the bigger the piles, the thinner the door. So what's an eerie, non-pastoral alternative to haystacks? I don't know. Probably not the time to be quibbling over imagery, anyway.

Where was I? Oh, the feeding slot. The feeding slot seemed like the only sensible thing to do. And the steaks do appear to appease them. There's a lot less scratching now. Of course, the mountain lions are still there. And the scratching and snuffling haven't stopped completely. They've just lessened. So I can't really say the problem is "solved."

Last week, I called the Department of Fish and Game. I asked if they could help me out. Maybe bring over a couple of those neck snare things. Like you see on those nature-man shows. Pull the lions out, bring them back to their native habitat, let them loose. They said it's not their problem either, though. Those guys and the construction foreman, two of a kind.

They also said this particular type of

mountain lion is endangered. Meaning, it's illegal to kill them. It would even be a felony if I let them die of neglect in my basement. Another reason to keep it up with the steaks.

Then I thought maybe, if they're so rare, I could make a few bucks off them. Sell them to a zoo. Nope. Selling them is a criminal offense, too. Endangered animal trafficking. And to top it off, word has gotten out to the animal rights people. A whole bunch of them are picketing out front. They're carrying signs with slogans:

Animal rights: no animal wronged.

Protect the lions' pride.

At first, I thought they might be of some help. Raise awareness and interest. Help get these animals back to the wild, right? Back where they belong, where they'll be more comfortable. But no, their position is exactly the opposite. The mountain lions have chosen to live in my basement. They should be allowed to remain. We've taken over their habitat, so now this is payback, etc. The activists insist they'll *intervene immediately* if I try anything that might harm the lions. Or anything that might infringe upon the lions' *inalienable rights*. Which apparently includes living in my basement.

So no help there, either.

I know it seems trivial, all other things considered, but did I mention about the laundry? The washer and dryer are in the basement. So we can't do laundry, considering the mountain lions. I know: we could go to a laundromat. But we just spent two grand on the new washer and dryer. And now I'm going to go and spend even more money to wash my clothes at a laundromat? In their inferior washing machines? With their harsh powdered detergents? In their non-adjustable oven-like dryers that will shrink all my clothes? That will burn my cashmere sweaters into charred husks of lint? That will transform my Egyptian poplin shirts into what? Into extremely expensive, nappy rags, fit only for doll costumes! Come on. I mean, really, come on. And then what will I wear to work when all my nice clothes are ruined? I'm a professional—an assistant professor of business mathematics. I can't go to work in a pair of greasy sweatpants. So, no. No, thank you. I will not throw my wardrobe away in those ill-maintained lint traps! Those churning boxes of imminent fire hazard! Gosh-damn-it-all to hell!

Wait, stop.

Deep breath.

I think I'm misplacing my anger about the mountain lions. Taking it out on the idea of laundromats. When in fact, I'm not angry at laundromats. Not really. Laundromats don't deserve that kind of badmouthing. They're perfectly productive businesses that provide a needed service to society. I just lost my head for a minute. Please excuse that outburst.

Anyway. If you have any idea what to do about the mountain lions, please let me know. I'm kind of at the end of my rope, here. Damned if I do, and all that. A felony to kill them, a felony to sell them, and a danger to keep them around. I mentioned that I have a baby son, right? And a wife? They can't defend themselves. Not against a hungry mountain lion. Much less against an unknown number of hungry and/or captivity-crazed mountain lions. And that door won't hold forever. I may have to take matters into my own hands, consequences be damned.

But not right now. Not yet. I don't want to do anything too rash, too hasty. Not until I've exhausted all my other options.

So, like I said: if you have any ideas, I'm open to suggestions.

For now, though, I'm headed to the supermarket. We're all out of steaks.

Souvenirs

It started with a few knickknacks—

A tiny model pickaxe embossed with the words *Yukon Territory.*

A brown bear statuette: standing up, brandishing the California flag.

A teacup-sized, ceramic covered wagon that reads *Oregon Trail: Westward Ho!*

I noticed them all one day, on a bookshelf in my bedroom, and I assumed my mother must have sent them, mementos from her post-retirement pilgrimages. Trips I had heard about during rambling phone conversations while I did my hair and makeup and got ready for work, or sat and ate a quick, microwaved dinner with a half-glass of wine, checking my email while she prattled on.

I thought, in the perpetually busy and distracted bustling of days—between bad dates, and long hours at the office, and endless trips to conferences—I must have opened packages containing these objects, set them out on display, and then promptly forgotten about them—only to find them again later as if for the first time.

Like I said, it started with the knickknacks—easy enough things to misplace or forget about or receive without even registering.

But then, a while later, there was an end table.

It was one of those integrated coffee-table-and-floor-lamp-in-one deals that looked straight from the seventies with a gilt-edged glass top, four lathe-turned wooden legs, and a green-shaded bulb.

If I didn't know any better, I'd think that it (or one of its close relatives, at least) might have lived in my grandparents' house when I was growing up—the sort of thing that one of my cousins would have smashed his forehead against as a toddler. If he went seeking consolation, he'd have been chastised by some cigarette-wielding, liquor-swirling great-aunt. I can almost hear the rasping, *That's what you get for running in the house!*

But, how did it end up here—in my apartment?

No idea.

Next thing was a guitar.

To be clear: I don't play the guitar. I don't play anything. I have no real desire to learn, no particular ear for music. In other words, I have no *reason* to have acquired a guitar.

I had a boyfriend once who played, but I can't imagine he'd leave it here all this time, unnoticed until now.

It's an old, acoustic model—that much I know. Lustrous, honey-colored wood, with luminous swirls of mother of pearl on the long piece that runs up under the strings, and a warm, musty smell inside its cavity. The knobs that tighten the strings are gold-plated. I can see my face reflected in them: two neat little rows of cameos.

When I plucked at the corroded, coppery strings, they gave a satisfying, rattly twang.

But, of course, that's not my point. My point is: what is it doing in my apartment? I broke up with it—or, with the guy, who must have left it here—long ago.

And the list goes on, too—those are just some highlights.

The more I've looked, the more I've found my apartment full of things—cooking utensils, bath towels, old clothes, plastic toys, framed photos, scented candles, paperback and hardcover books—that I can't remember picking out, that I'm sure I never bought, that I don't recall receiving, but that somehow made their way into my already-tiny living space, making it impossibly smaller.

It wasn't such an issue at first. But lately, with the pileup, I can hardly sit down or walk from bedroom to bathroom without climbing over piles or shoving things out of the way.

The largest recent arrival was an armoire.

That's right: an armoire.

How exactly one of those arrives unannounced, I couldn't begin to guess, but I woke up on Sunday to find it half-blocking the doorway to the kitchen. I stubbed three toes on it stumbling through to make coffee. When I pulled open its doors, I was nearly knocked backward by an avalanche of mothballed business suits, faded military uniforms, grass-stained overalls, and a whole slew of cable-knit wool cardigans from New Zealand. From the plackets and toggles and lapels, gold buttons and hooks winked up at me in the slanting, mid-morning light, like we shared some obscure half-secret.

I think the armoire is made of cherry wood. It's beautiful, really, and it smells like cedar and sage. But despite its charm, it's maybe not so practical for the space: It takes up a full third of the living room, so I've had to push the couch way back into the corner.

Then again, whether I want it or not, I have no idea how I'd ever get it out of here. It would never fit through the front door—at least not in one piece.

All else being equal, and other concerns aside, I do have this to say in its defense: It goes nicely with the antique sideboard that showed up yesterday—big as a coffin—overspread with huge, dust-greyed doilies. The sideboard's wide drawers are packed full of tarnished, hand-monogrammed flatware, delicate gold-leaf peeling from the engraved letters—three initials that, though I can't quite place them, feel vaguely, distantly familiar.

The World on Fire

Look, I know you're wondering why I'm dressed like this. You're thinking, *Hey, guy, what's with the red-and-orange robes?* And, *How come you've got soot smeared all over your face?* And, *Are those real feathers?*

Valid questions, for sure. So then, let me just explain, okay?

It all started with a surgery. A LaserTEK Corrective Laser Eye Surgery. LaserTEK is basically like Lasik, but more budget-conscious. And sure, in retrospect, laser eye surgery was probably not the thing to save a buck on. But we learn these lessons through experience, don't we? Anyway, I have mostly good things to say about LaserTEK. Nice people. Friendly service. Great results. Mostly.

I feel like I should mention: Before the surgery, I was practically blind. Couldn't tell my mother's face from a stranger's at ten paces, no exaggeration. Not like I'm old or anything, either—twenty-nine in May. Just drew bad numbers in the genetic lotto. It was so bad, for a while I wore glasses and contacts both at once. Even then I couldn't read without giving myself a headache.

So after the surgery, I was thrilled: the whole world snapped suddenly into focus. Like, really crisp, crystal-clear focus—I can't stress that enough—really incredible. I said *Good-bye, glasses! Catch ya later, contacts!* It was a total transformation of my eyesight experience—just like the brochures advertised. Among the many things I was amazed to discover: I could spot a familiar face from a half a block away; I could read the most miniscule text on my tablet—even at arm's length; I could make out the finest of fine print on any pill bottle or legal document; And I could see shimmering auras of golden flames flickering around everything in sight.

Understand, when I say I *could* see flames, I mean I *couldn't not* see them. They were literally everywhere I looked. The flames were not part of the advertised experience—I could find no mention of them anywhere in the literature, not even in the long list of possible side effects—and yet, there they were, looking as real, and as clear, and as hot as you can imagine. So right away I called Dr. Goodman, my LaserTEK Personal Eye-Care Consultant.

When Dr. Goodman picked up, it sounded like he was eating potato chips. There was a continuous, loud munching sound and intermittent, foily crinkling. He said he didn't think the surgery was to blame for the flames. In hundreds of patients, he had never heard of such a thing. He asked me if I had any history of mental illness or hallucinations, which I didn't.

Then he asked if I had signed all the indemnity waivers, which I had. He sounded pretty relieved about that. And then he asked how my vision was otherwise—*aside* from the hallucinatory flames.

I told him it was good—really, it was great—better than great—but the flames—!

Well then, Steve, I'd have to say I count the surgery a success, he said.

Yes, but—, I said.

Stay calm. I'm sure it'll fade. It's probably just a matter of time, he said.

He encouraged me to remind myself it was just a *minor optical disturbance*. As he spoke, I glanced around the room, squinting and unsquinting my eyes. On the counter, a flame-wreathed apple blurred and refocused. Yes, I thought: 'disturbance' is definitely the word for it.

After I hung up the phone, I paced around my apartment—a nervous habit. Mid-pace, I caught my reflection in the hall mirror and gasped at what I saw. My round, freckled face; short, brown hair; sloped, bony shoulders— all haloed in blazes. Jesus, I thought. If seeing himself burning alive isn't enough to scare a guy silly, I don't know what is.

As hours passed, the flames persisted. Despite Dr. Goodman's reassurances, I grew increasingly edgy and anxious. I felt an unfamiliar, uncomfortable sense of urgency. I'd say it sprung from a dawning awareness of the extraordinary preciousness of time—but maybe that's getting too flowery with it. Really, it was more like every minute I had ever wasted watching bad TV—or playing mindless video games, or reading blogs, or indulging in self-obsessed fantasies—came back to haunt me like cheap Chinese food. I wondered: What had I done with my invaluable time—where had it gone? And, perhaps more importantly, what did I have to show for it?

I made a brief attempt to distract myself from these thoughts by reading a book. But since the book, too, appeared to be on fire, that didn't really help. Too demoralized to resort to TV or the Internet, I tried an improvised mantra:

It's only an illusion—an optical disturbance.
It's only an illusion—an optical disturbance.
It's only an illusion—an optical disturbance.

That gave me something to focus on, and it sounded soothingly officious. But the technique was flawed, because as soon as my concentration faltered—as soon as my attention slipped even slightly from the syllables—I slid back into the snug wrapping of angst that was quickly becoming my new norm. I glanced, inevitably, at one object or another—a bookshelf that blazed like a hearth; a toothbrush that flared like an oversized matchstick—and any bit of cool, calm reason went immediately up in smoke. It's no coincidence that the old saying goes: *seeing is believing.* What I was seeing was Windex-clear and pee-your-pants terrifying.

The whole world on fire.

That afternoon, I stood in line at GroceryPlus fretting with my shirt cuffs. To my left: racks of magazines, engulfed; to my right: cartons of candy, blazing. I had gone to the store because I usually found grocery shopping calming. Typically, the long, orderly rows of neatly stacked packages had a pacifying effect. But this time, the whole thing had a frantic, harried feeling. I ran through the store, haphazardly grabbing milk, bacon, a dozen eggs. In my haste, I knocked over an elaborate display of cereal boxes.

Of course, conceptually, I still knew the flames weren't real—but I couldn't shake the sensation. At the checkout stand, I couldn't understand: Why did it take such an ungodly long time to ring up a basket of groceries? And how did no one else appear to be in a hurry? In front of me, an old woman handed coupons to the distracted, gum-popping cashier—one by excruciatingly slow one. Unable to wait any longer, I set down my basket of unbought groceries and left the store.

Emerging into the burning daylight, I paused for a moment to consider my options. I thought about heading to the Village Centre, to stop in at Java Joe's. I'd been working there as a barista the past two years while part-timing my way to an MA in English at Odsburg College. Maybe I'd go tell my boss, Terri, that I quit. No more hustling for beans. But then I found myself wondering, *Why bother?* If the flames were real, the whole place would be French roast soon anyway. And even if they weren't real, weren't there better things I could do? Time was wasting, and I had wasted enough of it already.

And then, as I stood there, it came to me: one thing I could do, before the whole burning world—not really, I knew—but still, maybe?—no, no, not really—don't be ridiculous, Steve—but, then again, possibly?—crumbled to ashes.

I headed downtown. Among the shops on Main Street, I ducked in and out of a jeweler's. Then I walked west along Hickory Avenue;

I turned north on Sycamore Street. Into the residential district: Dutch Elm Drive, Juniper Terrace, Knotty Pine Lane. Soon I was passing between green-lawned homes and the blacktop aprons of apartments. Gradually, I broke from a fast walk into a jog into a sprint. As I sped up, the blazing facades of the brick-and-shingle buildings roared past on either side. Up above, clusters of flame-laden clouds hung hot in the sky.

Will—you—marry—me?

I punctuated the question with sharp, gasping breaths. I had sprinted the two miles to my girlfriend Allison's apartment. Bursting in—panting, sweating, wild-eyed—I can only imagine what I looked like. Shivers, Allison's gray-and-white tabby, ran yowling into the bedroom. Allison, herself, was caught off-guard. She was also, to my view, caught on fire. That image was only intensified by the usual sheen of her reddish curls. I resisted the powerful urge to swat her with a blanket, or push her to the floor and roll her over and over. Instead, I did what I'd come to do. From my pocket I pulled a small, velvet box—opened it—held it out. I dropped to one knee and a desperate smile seeped across my face. Allison didn't speak, or blink, for several seconds.

Her jaw fell open to reveal a little pool of fire lapping around the edges of her tongue. Finally she spoke, very quietly.

Steve, what are you doing?

I told her I was seizing the day.

Seriously, she said. *What's this about? Do you feel okay? You look flushed.*

I told her I felt incredible—more alive than ever! I told her closeness to death breeds appreciation for the vivid beauty of life. Allison pressed a forefinger to her lip as she looked at me for another long moment.

You're scaring me, she said. *Also, there's no ring in the box.*

I blushed—embarrassed, but not deterred—and conceded: true, there was no ring. This seemed to bring her some tiny bit of relief. At least I was *aware* that I had just proposed with an empty box. I told her I didn't have time to pick out a ring, but for obvious reasons (reasons that were obvious only to me, as I hadn't filled her in on my predicament) I didn't want to wait any longer to propose. I told her I wanted to do something real, something substantial. It could be the last thing I ever did. Then I added that I wanted to be a father, too, but that was more of a long-term investment, and who knew: did we really have that much time on the table? Seeing that she still looked anxious, I told her not to worry: I would get the ring later. If there *was* a later.

But what's the rush? She said. *We've got plenty of time. Besides, I'm not ready.*

I asked her, if she wasn't ready then, then when—*when*!? At this, Allison shrugged.

A couple years. After we finish grad school, find jobs, save a little money.

My response was not so much actual words, but more of a gagging sound. I meant to indicate that we likely didn't have that long. I decided to try reasoning with her—to help her see the light. So I told her what I saw: everything burning. And I told her what it meant: our time might run out any minute. And I shouted it a second time for emphasis: *Any minute!*

She was clearly thinking about what I had said: her forehead broke into flaming furrows. After a brief pause, she said she knew, in a sense, that I was right.

As soon as we're born we start dying, right? No one knows how much time we have?

Is that what you mean?

But I was impatient: I could tell she wasn't feeling the same urgency. For her it was abstract, conceptual—just ideas. *Life is fleeting. Time is precious.* Whereas for me, it was immediate, concrete, and utterly real. *Your head is on fire. Your cat is on fire. Your neighbors' house, through the window behind you, is on fire.* There was nothing abstract about it. I told Allison I couldn't talk about it anymore—I needed to go. Suddenly I'd had another idea.

I encouraged her to think about the proposal. But if I'm being honest, I knew then we were through. Quite literally, we no longer saw things the same. I needed someone who was ready to commit—no more delays. Plus, if that weren't enough, she'd never have stayed with me like this: dressed like some weird animal, standing out on a street corner all day. I see myself for what I am, I really do. No job, no stability, dubious sanity. It's not exactly the 'complete package' that women yearn for. Takes a special kind to love this. But anyway, I'm getting off course.

I kissed Allison goodbye, turned on one heel, and started off down the street running back in the direction from which I'd come. Over my shoulder, I cast a parting glance. She stood there, still stunned, flames dancing around her head like cartoon stars. Shivers crouched between her feet, fastidiously grooming. He was taking his time, licking thin tendrils of fire from between his toes.

Let me say this now, to save you the trouble later: I knew my idea was a long shot—a fool's errand, really—but I felt I had to try it. Maybe I can cite temporary insanity or something, like they do in court? Because you're going to laugh when I tell you what I did. Why would it ever work, right? But just think about it. If you were seeing flames everywhere, would rationality really be front and center? Or would you maybe try anything— even something crazy—out of sheer desperation? Judge not unless you're ready to be judged is all I'm saying. Walk a mile in my shoes and all that.

So anyway, I ran as fast as I could back toward the center of town—my lungs and legs, like everything else, burning. When I neared my destination, I scrambled to a halt, huffing and puffing. I looked up at the face of the large, square, brick building. Two massive garage bay doors stood open like a pair of startled eyes.

I walked into one of the open bays and my hand stretched up toward a gleaming chrome handle on a polished red door—rising as if enchanted, as if commanded, as if magnetized. But before I reached the handle, I felt a big, meaty palm land on my shoulder. I spun around to find myself face-to-face with a uniformed fireman: black boots, brown pants, red suspenders, and a navy blue t-shirt. Out of the t-shirt, the man's neck and biceps bulged gratuitously. Wisps of flame hovered around them, barely escaping his collar and cuffs. His t-shirt was embroidered with the name *Ted*.

Can I help you? said Ted the fireman.

I asked him for a tour of the station and said I'd like to become a volunteer.

He stared hard at me and raised an eyebrow. *Oh*, he said. *Really?*

Admittedly, I'm not a burly guy: I don't look the part of the fireman. I tried taking a deep breath and inflating my chest to maximize my size. A number of animals do this, with some success, in the wild. But as I exhaled and deflated, my heart dipped: I feared I would lose my chance. So I told Ted I was stronger than I looked, and to prove it, I proposed a bet. I bet him I could unroll the fire hose all by myself—and then, further, that I could hold it steady, single-handedly, on full-blast.

Ted looked at me like a horn had sprouted from my forehead. I suggested we put some money on it—a hundred bucks. If I could do it, he'd pay up; if not, then he was that much richer. At first, he looked like he'd have no part of it. He shook his hamlike head and made some pronouncements about protocols and safety. But with a little more prodding—and wondering aloud what harm it could do when Ted would be standing right there the whole time, ready to defuse any possible complication—he seemed to soften. He admitted that the rest of the crew was on a call and would be gone awhile. He rubbed his palms together and interlaced his thick fingers. Heat ripples rose from the lattice of his hands, like the shimmer above a barbecue pit. Slowly, he nodded and then gave a little shrug.

Okay, sure, he said. *What the hell.*

Within a few minutes, I had spun the hose off the spool. It trailed along the pavement in long, cursive loops. I walked the length of it, removing curls and kinks, until it formed a straight, white line. By this time, I was exhausted: I was breathing heavy and my muscles ached. I was afraid of what would happen when the hose filled with water, but I wasn't about to waste this opportunity. I lifted the nozzle and looked back at Ted expectantly. He pulled a second, shorter hose from another spool and attached it to a forked spigot protruding from the station's front wall. Then he walked back over and turned a wheel on the side of the truck. He warned me to get ready—to make sure I had a nice, solid grip.

Once it picks up, he said, *it's a real sonofagun to handle*.

I watched as the hose filled with water, inflated like the world's largest balloon animal. Then it snapped taut like a flexed bicep and immediately sprang from my grasp. As it left my hands, it knocked me hard on the chin. I stood there, dazed, and watched as it danced. It swayed and shimmied like a drunk python, drenching whatever it faced.

At first, I was jubilant: my plan had worked! I followed the stream of water, desperate to see the flames extinguished. My eyes flashed from one point to another as the water changed directions. It splashed the sidewalk—then a passing car— then a row of bushes alongside the firehouse— then fireman Ted, as he scrambled to corral the hose's erratic movements.

My hopes, however, were quickly doused. The flames continued to flicker, even as the water washed over. Then, with a further pang of horror, I realized something else: the water itself was being lapped by the flames. In a frantic, final effort, I sprinted past soggy-burning Ted and darted into the truck bay. I grabbed a handheld fire extinguisher off the wall and sprayed it on the sidewalk. To my disgusted unsurprise, the foam, like everything else, was coated in flame.

So my plan had failed.

In its wake came a kind of welcome resignation. After I had exhausted my storehouse of grasping panic—after I had given up on trying to do anything and everything before time ran out—after the emotional storm—came an unforeseen, great calm. Standing on the sidewalk, with my erstwhile-clenched jaw slackened—with my formerly tense arms hanging loosely at my sides—looking at the wildly spewing water and the spent, sticky foam—watching Ted shut off the valve, the hose pinned under his hulking frame—witnessing the life slowly draining from the deanimated hose—my tone, my tenor, my internal temperature, suddenly cooled. I said to myself, over and over:

Everything is burning.
Everything is burning.
Everything is burning.

But I no longer felt as if my mind, itself, was on fire. I realized, yes, everything was burning—and yet, somehow, everything was not burned. Despite the flames, the world was not in ruin. The tension in my body drained further until even my eyes relaxed. My focus softened until all I could see was a big, orange blur. And then slowly, there on the sidewalk in the midst of everything, I shut my eyes. Behind my lids, the flames did not follow me—not completely. Instead, they formed a burned-in afterglow, a negative trace. Like when you've stared too directly at the sun. The glow resolved gradually into a tufted crest, two broad wings, and a curling, paisley tail. Bright against black, this strange bird wafted. Its wings flapped gently, leaving their own fiery trails. And suddenly I realized what I had seen was not a world destined for the ashcan. It was a zoo full of phoenixes in all stages of death and rebirth. Everything burning, and everything forged anew from that same fire. Yes, I thought, it will all give way and dissolve into the flames, eventually. But it will come out, not just destroyed, but transformed.

Metamorphosis.

A world in perpetual transition.

A great carousel of living and dying.

A truly—well, you get the point, right?

No need to beat it to death.

So I've been out here every day since, spreading that message, speaking my truth. I just feel like I have no choice but to tell people what I've seen. Such a beautiful image, isn't it—full of pathos, but also filled with hope? It really highlights the beauty and the fragility, and ultimately, the resilience of life. Or something like that, anyway. Of course, beauty aside, this gig doesn't put food in my stomach. Because everybody's got to eat, right? And my lawsuit against LaserTEK is looking like a dead end. Last I checked, their 800 number was disconnected and their Web domain had lapsed.

I guess what I'm trying to say is, anything you can spare is appreciated. Drop it right here in my feathered hat, please—yes, thank you, thanks, I really mean it. That's great.

Mel and the Microphones

Microphones. Microphones. Microphones.

In the kitchen, microphones. In the bathroom, microphones. In the bedroom, microphones. In the garage and the office and the den and the great room; in the laundry room and the breakfast nook and the dining room; in the guest bedroom and the foyer and the mudroom; in the backyard and the front yard and the side yard and the driveway; in the car and the half-bath and the patio. Microphones.

None of them are live. None of them plugged in. None of them even with cords running out of them. None with batteries. No little glowing green lights. No functioning microphones whatsoever. Some of the microphones aren't even really microphones. Some of the microphones are tea strainers—the kind with the silvery metal mesh ball on the end of a wire stick—stuck into an empty toilet paper tube and then wrapped with duct tape, looking passingly like a microphone if you squint. Or have bad eyesight. Or if you aren't looking too closely. Or maybe only catch it in your peripheral vision. Some of the microphones are toys or pictures printed on plain white copy paper. Microphones and fake microphones and images of microphones. All over. All over the house.

My husband Mel is senile. Has advanced dementia. He's eighty-five years old. Used to be a sportscaster. A play-by-play announcer. His whole career. Forty-plus years. Highly respected. Widely known.

And then there's me: Karen. Me: The devoted wife. My hair gone sheer white. Married five decades. Our four children all grown. Kids of their own. Busy living in far off cities. And me:

still here haunting this old, echoing Victorian. Me: left with nothing to do but watch and wait and wonder. Me: remembering everything. My mind still clear, still sharp.

But Mel, he forgets.

I got the idea to set up the microphones when I noticed him one afternoon, talking a mile a minute into one of my hairbrushes. That's how this all got started.

And the chicken is cooking, browning, sizzling!
Folks, this is going to be a dinner for the ages!
Oh my, that's the buzzer. Stick a fork in it.
It. Is. Done!

Before the microphones Mel wouldn't say two words all day. But with a mic—or something that looks passably *similar* to a mic—he'll talk day in and day out. 'Til he's hoarse. 'Til I turn off the lights and go to bed. And sometimes he'll keep right on after that. I don't mind, even when it keeps me up nights—it's better than the quiet.

Play-by-play, though it's not conversation exactly, is far better than nothing.

Most importantly, it makes me feel like my husband is still here. Like he's still alive, still my husband. Anyway, more so than I felt during the long, staring, drooling hours before.

They're on the couch, watching television!
They've finished two programs.
I think they might go for three!
What a night, folks. What. A. Night!

Phil Fleming was Mel's commentating partner. They worked together, side-by-side, for thirty-two years. A long, successful marriage in its own right. Phil's dead now, has been for more than a decade. When Mel gets going, he often speaks to Phil. It makes me sad, because it breaks the illusion that my husband is truly lucid—the impression that he's really talking to me. But then, so does the fact that he's commentating on all of life's little occurrences. As if they were major sporting events. As if they warranted this type of ticker tape narration.

Narration that reminds me of the grandkids' constant, chirpy self-commentary on their social media apps, their mobile devices. The kind of chatter that says, *I'm here, I'm here, I'm here*. The kind that reassures the speaker that she's alive. If only because she can hear herself talking.

As if all the little moments—all the tiny details of your life—deserved attention, and documentation, and broadcast.

This is it folks.
It's the moment we've all been waiting for!
She's putting on rouge!
She's spraying on the Aqua-Net!
She's taking out her rollers!
It's all coming down to this, folks!
And she could be—is she?

Yes—she's ready for a night on the town!

BFF

Carl shuffled in and slumped down across from me at the café table. He was dressed for the office, but at eight in the morning already disheveled. The front of his blue Oxford shirt was rumpled, rain-speckled, half-untucked. His gray, pinstriped tie hung loose, crumpled like a downed kite. Stray hairs stuck up at odd angles around his bald spot. His wire-frames were slightly askew and kept sliding down the sweat-slick slope of his nose. It was clear from his jerky movements he was nervous.

I said:

Hey, how you doing?
You okay, Carl?

I said: **He said:**

Hello, Vernon, thanks for meeting me here.

Of course. What are friends for?

Friends—right—we are—certainly have been.

You're acting weird, Carl. Is something wrong?

Well, the thing is—the thing is—

His voice caught in his throat. He looked down at his hands, clenched into tight, white fists. Then he started again.

I said:

Come on, Carl.
Whatever it is, just
say it!

He said:

The thing is, I'm pretty
sure—that is to say,
I suspect—I mean, I
think—

Okay, I've determined,
Vernon, that you're,
well, that you're
imaginary.

Wait. What?

You're not real—you're
an illusion, produced
by my mind.

I know what
'imaginary' means.

Well then, what's the
confusion?

I said:

He said:

*How can you suggest
I'm imaginary when
I'm sitting here talking
to you!?*

*Doctor Weiss told me
you might ask that—*

Doctor Wise?

My psychiatrist.

I don't believe this.

*And it's Weiss, not
'Wise'—W-e-i-s-s—a
soft 's.'*

At that point Carl didn't say anything for a few moments. He sat there wringing his hands and staring at the fake wood grain on the tabletop. Then he swallowed hard like a skinny snake with a fat hamster in his throat.

He said:

*Look, Vernon, there's
something more—and
please don't interrupt.*

*This is hard for
me. You need to
understand.*

*But I think it would be
best if you would stop
appearing.*

*It's unhealthy—to keep
talking to you like this.*

*I'm thirty-eight, for
Chrissakes. It's—it's—
maladaptive.*

I said:

Maladaptive.

*You know what that
sounds like?*

*A fancy doctor
word—a word you
wouldn't have used
before!*

*Like you're just
regurgitating what
Doctor Weiss-sssss tells
you!*

Do you know what
that *word means,
Carl—'regurgitating'?*

I said:

It means throwing up!
Vomiting! Spitting out
undigested!

As in, 'You're making
me so sick I'm about to
regurgitate all over the
table.'

I was off on a bit of a rant, I admit. But then I saw the look on Carl's face—so pitiful, so forlorn. His eyes turned glossy behind his glasses. And I realized he didn't *want* to do this: the doctor had put him up to it. So I tried a different approach.

Let's just hold on a
minute—not lose our
heads prematurely,
okay?

I said:

*Think about it: we've
been through so much
together, Carl, you and
me.*

*In and out of trouble
together so many
times—since we were
kids!*

*The time you drew on
the walls and blamed
it on me, but your
mom didn't buy it.*

*And in third grade,
when you threw
cottage cheese at Ricky
Noonan?*

I said:　　　　　　　**He said:**

You got sent to the principal's, and I sat with you all afternoon!

And in high school, when we rode a shopping cart into the lake.

You nearly drowned— you could have died!

Who dragged you out and kept you conscious 'til the paramedics arrived?　　　*You did, but—*

Ooh, and the trip to Howe Caverns!

I said:

*When we were
befriended-slash-
attacked by a family
of bats.*

*Or the rough patch I
helped you through,
when Amy broke up
with you.*

*And we TP'ed her yard
and dropped dog turds
on her porch.*

*And she threatened a
restraining order.*

I said:

He said:

And we went for a consolatory comfort food binge at the Golden Corral!

Yeah—

Or—or—the time you were accused of embezzling from the credit union.

I stayed home with you to watch game shows and eat Cheetos all day.

Those whole two months while you were on administrative leave!

I know—

I said:

*Until your name was
finally cleared and you
were allowed to return
to work!*

*You don't think I had
other things to do?—
other places to be?*

*But I was there for
you, Carl, and I never
regretted a minute of
it.*

*I could go on for
hours—there are just
so many memories!*

He said:

Yeah, we've had some times—been through a lot together, that's for sure.

Remembering all that, Carl smiled. Then he was smiling and crying at the same time. And then my eyes started welling up, too. Right about then a waitress came around to the table. Her nametag said 'Jennette.' Seeing her coming, Carl wiped the tears off his face with a napkin.

She said:

Can I get you anything?

Yes. Two tall coffees. One for me, and one for my imaginary friend.

Let me tell you: the look Jennette gave Carl, when he said '*one for my imaginary friend.*' She looked so skeptical, so hesitant—afraid, even—like she thought Carl was crazy. Like she didn't believe for a second that I was imaginary. Like she could see me there, plain as day, and knew I was one-hundred-percent real. That look was very reassuring—I could have hugged good ol' Jennette for that. I didn't—but I could have.

She said:

Um, sure, okay.

Then she walked away, quickly. When she came back a minute later, she set two coffees on the table, side-by-side. Then she speed-walked away again. After Jennette left, Carl turned back to me. He looked me straight in the eye this time.

I said:

He said:

*Look, Vernon, you've
been there for me
through thick and
thin.*

*And I appreciate it—I
really do—but the
thing is—*

*There's no denying—no
getting around the
fact—*

*You're an aberration—
a mental projection—
and it's not healthy—*

*Jesus, again with the
psychobabble—don't
listen to that doctor,
listen to how you feel.*

For a moment, he looked conflicted. He tugged his left earlobe and frowned.

I said:

He said:

No offense—I feel I'd like to be a normal guy with normal real-person friends.

No offense!

Carl looked around the café like he was suddenly worried what people might think. As for me, I was definitely taking offense. He could claim all day that I'm imaginary, but the pain, the heartbreak, the betrayal—the hurt I felt in that moment? It was real. Of course, I didn't want Carl to know how much he'd wounded me. So I went with anger instead.

Screw you, Carl, screw you!

Keep it down, Vernon—

I said:

*What do I care? I'm
not real, remember?
How can I care what
anybody thinks?*

He said:

*You're making a
scene—people are
starting to stare.*

*Just calm down,
Vernon. Please just
calm down.*

He made a 'calming' gesture with his hands. It looked like he was pressing down on something invisible in front of him. Trying to stuff it under the table. He looked around again. People were definitely staring. Suddenly, I had an idea. I leaned across the table and lowered my voice to a whisper.

*Carl, how do you know
Doctor Weiss is real?*

Well—

Well?

I said:

He said:

I guess maybe I don't know for sure.

So why let a maybe-maladaptive-figment-doctor turn you against your best friend?

But I did see his medical license and diploma.

So?

And he spoke to his secretary, so either they're both imaginary—

Which is possible.

Or, they're both real.

He squinted and looked me hard in the face for a moment. Something about that look—I didn't like it.

I said:

He said:

Now I think about it, Vern, I've never seen anyone else talk to you.

I'm just an introvert— people can sense that.

And look, you're not even drinking your coffee! I bet you can't.

Sure I can—I just have a long drive and don't want to have to pee.

Oh yeah? What kind of car do you drive?

I hesitated, trying to come up with the name of a real car that real people drive. It's funny, the little details that make all the difference in the world. The difference, for example, between keeping and losing your best and only friend. I kicked myself for not noticing any of the names on the cars in the parking lot outside. Finally, I decided to take a guess; too much hesitation, and I'd have lost him anyway. I said I drove a Ford Tuberous—I thought it sounded plausible. Carl's eyes flashed. He looked triumphant.

I said:

He said:

There's no such thing!

Fine! Fine! I guess you got me, then.

I guess I did.

Then, after a couple seconds, his face fell. He sucked in a deep breath and blew it out with a sigh. His shoulders slumped and he leaned back into his chair. His exuberance was replaced by a kind of sad-but-satisfied resolve. And that's when I knew it was really over. So I gave him a little parting speech—a speech that I think was pretty good, especially considering it was totally off-the-cuff, without notes or anything.

I said:

*You don't want me
around anymore, that's
fine.*

*I'll find someone else to
spend my time with,
because you know
what, Carl?*

I said:

*You suck! You suck suck
suck suck suck!*

*I guess I'll go hang
out with the Tooth
Fairy—or the Loch
Ness Monster.*

*Or some other people
you don't believe are
real—how about that?*

*I'll throw a party and
invite everybody—
gnomes!—bigfoots!—
Martians!*

*Anyway, there's no use
hanging around here.*

I said:

Because if there's one
thing I've learned, it's
to not stick around
where I'm not wanted.

And one more thing,
Carl: It's your loss!

Then I got up from my seat and I walked to the door of the café. I left the coffee sitting there on the table to show Carl I didn't want his charity. And I waited, stubbornly, with my back to Carl, until a pretty young woman opened the door. Then I ducked underneath her arm and slipped out silently, into the drab, drizzly morning. As I walked away, I glanced back just once to see Carl sitting there, still inside the café—alone at a table for two, with two cups of coffee getting cold.

Acknowledgements

The following stories from this collection have been previously published in the following places:

"The Water Cycle" in *New Haven Review*

"Seeking Advice and/or Assistance re: Mountain Lions" in *Post Road*

"Souvenirs" in *Transverse Journal*

"The World on Fire" in *Little Patuxent Review*

"Mel and the Microphones" in *Atticus Review*

"BFF" in *Firewords Quarterly*

About the Author

Matt Tompkins is the author of *Studies in Hybrid Morphology*, out now from tNY Press. Matt's stories have appeared in *Little Patuxent Review*, *New Haven Review*, *Post Road*, and other journals. He works in a library and lives in upstate New York with his wife (who kindly reads his first drafts), his daughter (who prefers picture books), and his cat (who is illiterate).